Monkeys
and the Universe

Kate Banks
Pictures by **Tomek Bogacki**

Frances Foster Books
Farrar, Straus and Giroux New York

To Pluto, which has been
reclassified as a dwarf planet
—K.B. and T.B.

Text copyright © 2009 by Kate Banks
Pictures copyright © 2009 by Tomek Bogacki
All rights reserved
Distributed in Canada by Douglas & McIntyre Ltd.
Color separations by Chroma Graphics PTE Ltd.
Printed and bound in China by South China Printing Co. Ltd.
Designed by Irene Metaxatos
First edition, 2009
1 3 5 7 9 10 8 6 4 2

www.fsgkidsbooks.com

Library of Congress Cataloging-in-Publication Data
Banks, Kate, date.
Monkeys and the universe / Kate Banks ; pictures by Tomek Bogacki.— 1st ed.
    p. cm.
Summary: Max and his older brother Pete learn about stars, planets, and
galaxies when their father takes them to an astronomical observatory.
ISBN-13: 978-0-374-35028-4
ISBN-10: 0-374-35028-0
[1. Astronomy—Fiction. 2. Astronomical observatories—Fiction.
3. Brothers—Fiction.] I. Bogacki, Tomasz, ill. II. Title.

PZ7.B22594 Mon 2009
[E]—dc22

2006048401

Contents

A Speck in the Universe   4

Cosmic Chaos   12

Great Galaxies   20

Twinkle, Twinkle, Little Star   42

A Speck in the Universe

Max stood outside his big brother Pete's room. There was a sign tacked to the door. DO NOT ENTER, it read.

"May I come in?" asked Max.

"Not unless you know the password," said Pete.

Max thought of Pete's favorite sport. "Basketball?" he said.

"Nope," said Pete.

He thought of Pete's favorite food. "Strawberries?" he said.

"Nope," said Pete again. "But I'll give you a clue. It's the name of the planet farthest from the sun."

"Neptune," said Max.

"Okay," said Pete. "You can come in."

Pete was making something. He had paper, glue, scissors, paint, and some Styrofoam balls. It looked fun.

"What are you doing?" asked Max.
"Can I help?"

"I'm making a model of our solar system," said Pete. "These are the planets." Pete named them. "Mercury, Venus, Earth, Mars, Jupiter, Saturn, Uranus, and Neptune. They revolve around the sun."

"Where's the moon?" asked Max.
"Isn't that part of the universe?"

"Here," said Pete, picking up a smaller ball. "It revolves around the earth, and it sometimes gets hit by asteroids, meteors, and comets."

Max sighed. Pete sure knew a lot.

"Some people think the moon is made of cheese," said Max. He had thought so when he was younger.

"Well, they're wrong," said Pete. "Just because something looks like Swiss cheese doesn't mean it is. Those holes are just a bunch of craters."

Pete patted Max on the shoulder. "The moon is two thousand miles across," he said. "You know what that makes you? A speck in the universe."

Max didn't like being the little brother in the family. Now Pete was calling him a speck. Max hated that.

"I'm not a speck," he said.

"I'm afraid you are," said Pete.

Cosmic Chaos

Max went to the kitchen. All that talk about cheese had made him hungry.

"What's up?" said his mother. She had just finished making strawberry jam.

"Nothing much," said Max. He spread some jam on a slice of bread and gobbled it up.

It filled his tummy and made him feel less like a speck.

"Max," said his mom, "could you reach under the counter? I dropped the top to the jam jar."

"Why don't you ask Pete?" said Max.

"Pete's too big," said his mom. "You're just the right size."

"You mean small," said Max. He got the top for his mother. She screwed it back on the jar.

"Did you know the sun is really a star?" asked Max. He'd learned that at school.

"I did," said his mom.

"Oh," said Max. Why did everyone have to know everything before he did?

Max went back upstairs. He passed
Pete's room. The door was open. Pete was
humming. Max started humming, too.

"Hey," said Pete. "I thought you
wanted to help."

Max picked up the tube of glue. He
gave it a squeeze.

"You can pass me the scissors," said
Pete.

"I want to paint," said Max.

"You'll mess everything up," said Pete. "Just give me the scissors."

"I won't wreck anything," said Max. He looked at the planet Saturn. It had a giant cardboard ring around it. Max picked it up.

"Put that down," said Pete.

"I'm just looking at the universe," said Max.

"If you touch another thing, I'll send you into another universe," said Pete.

For a moment, Max thought he might be better off in another universe.

"See you later," he said.

Great Galaxies

Max went to his room and took out his box of marbles. He began building his own solar system. He used a red marble for Mars, a blue marble for Venus, and a green marble for Earth. Then he put himself in the center. "I'll be the sun," he thought.

Suddenly a ball sailed past Max's head and knocked the green marble out of the solar system.

"Uh-oh," said Pete. "A meteorite just banged into planet Earth."

Max went to Pete's room. He took the
planet Neptune from Pete's model and
tossed it out the window.

"Hey, what are you doing?" cried Pete.

"Didn't you say Neptune was the
farthest planet from the sun?" said Max.

"Go get it," shouted Pete.

"No!" cried Max.

"Yes!" screamed Pete.

"What's going on here?" shouted their dad, who'd been mowing the lawn.

"Pete destroyed planet Earth," said Max.

"And Max sent Neptune out of the solar system," said Pete.

"I had a little surprise for you boys," said their dad. "But now that I find myself in the middle of Star Wars, I'm having second thoughts."

"Surprise?" said Pete. He returned Earth to Max's universe.

"What kind of surprise?" said Max. He went down to the garden to get Neptune.

Max and Pete got into the car.

"Where are we going?" asked Max.

"Give us just a little hint," said Pete.

"I'll only say that it's out of this world," said their dad.

"Sounds great," said Pete.

They pulled to a stop in front of a building with a large dome. It had no windows.

"Where are we?" asked Max.

"This is an observatory," said his dad.

"What's that?" asked Max.

"It's a place where people study the sky, the planets, and the stars," said his dad.

They went inside. A guide led them to
the room with the dome. Her name was
Stella. Max and Pete sat down next to
each other.

The room was like a movie theater with rows of seats.

"Cool," said Pete. Suddenly Stella's voice came over a loudspeaker.

"I'm sure you have all heard of the Milky Way," she said.

"It's a candy bar," whispered Max.

"A Milky Way is a candy bar," said Stella. "But it is also the name of our galaxy. A galaxy is a collection of stars. There are more than a billion galaxies in the universe."

"Wow," said Max.

Stella continued. "We talk about the stars coming out at night," she said. "But the stars are out all the time. We just don't see them during the day because the sky is too bright."

Suddenly the lights went out, and
above them the dome lit up with stars like
the nighttime sky.

"In our galaxy, stars are grouped
together in clusters called constellations."
Stella pointed to a group of stars shaped
like a big bear.

"That's the constellation of Ursa Major,"
she said. Then she pointed to another.
"And that's Orion, the hunter."

"Are there any monkeys?" whispered
Max.

"I don't think so," said Pete.

The lights flickered back on.

Stella took them into another room with charts and pictures. She pointed to a photo of a comet and explained that the word "comet" came from the Greek word for "hair."

"That tail we see is a trail of gas blown by the wind," she said. "But our ancestors thought that comets were stars with hair flowing behind them."

"Does anyone have a comb?" asked Pete. "I have to comb my comet."

Max laughed.

Stella led them into another room,
which had a big telescope.

Max and Pete took turns looking
through it. But they couldn't see much.
It wasn't dark enough.

"On a clear, dark night, you can see the rings of Saturn, and the red spot on Jupiter, which is actually a storm," said Stella.

"With a telescope you can see the colors of the stars," said their dad.

"Aren't stars yellow?" said Max.

"Not all of them," said Stella. "Stars can be blue, yellow, green, or red."

Max closed his eyes and imagined the sky sparkling like a box of jewels.

"May we come back and look through the telescope sometime when it's dark?" asked Pete.

"Sure," said his dad.

Max and Pete thanked Stella.

"My pleasure," she said. Then she gave them each a package of phosphorescent stars. "With these you can make your own constellations," she said.

Max climbed into the car next to Pete. He remembered something he'd read at school. "If we were driving to the sun, it would take us longer than one hundred years," he said.

"I didn't know that," said Pete. "We'd better get started then."

"Wait a minute," said Dad. "There's no homemade jam on the sun. I think we ought to just go home. What do you say?"

"Okay," said Max and Pete together.

Twinkle, Twinkle, Little Star

That evening, Max got ready for bed.
He stuck his stars on his bedroom
window.

His parents came in to say good night.

"See my constellation?" said Max. He'd
made a monkey face.

"Nice," said his mom.

Max looked out the window at the twinkling stars. "They're millions of miles away," he said.

"But they reach right into your bedroom," said Max's dad. "Amazing, isn't it?"

"The universe is really big," said Max.
He was feeling small again.

Max's mom and dad gave him a hug
and kissed him good night. Then they
turned out the lights.

Max looked back out the window at the stars. He could see the moon now, too. Pretty soon he heard footsteps. It was Pete.

"Are you asleep?" Pete asked.

"No," said Max.

"May I come in?" asked Pete.

"Sure," said Max.

Pete climbed into bed next to Max. "Sorry I destroyed your solar system," he said.

"It's okay," said Max. "I can make another one."

"I'll help," said Pete.

He pulled the covers up over both of them.

"You know, I'm glad we're part of the same universe," he said.

"Me too," said Max.